Tricia & Kitty

Still in Love

Their Kids are all grown up.
What's next?

R.L. ATKINS

Tricia & Kitty: Still in Love

This book is a work of fiction. People, places, events, and situations are the products of the authors imagination. Any resemblance to persons, living or dead, or historical events, are purely coincidental.

ISBN

Paperback	978-1-68547-153-8
Hardcover	978-1-68547-154-5
eBook	978-1-68547-155-2

Library of Congress Control Number: 2022915320
Printed in the United States of America

wordHOUSE

101 Foundry Dr,
West Lafayette, IN, 47906, USA

www.wordhousebp.com
+1-800-646-8124

TRICIA & KITTY

Still in Love

Trish and Kitty are still in love after all these years. Their children are the kind of kids that make you proud.

Their oldest son, Evan died a hero while on a mission for the CIA. His ashes are in a memorial garden at his New Mexico home where he grew up.

Their second oldest, Buddy, is a successful medical device engineer and lives near Kansas City. His wife, Brenda is a full blooded Apache from the Reservation in southern New Mexico. They met in College. They have a Son.

Their youngest adopted child is Patty. She opened a Dog grooming salon near Albuquerque. She has recently married her business partner and lover, Tina Frost.

They inherited a large fortune including a house and several cars from one of their Grooming clients. They had accompanied her to Dog shows to do grooming on her dog. They also inherited her Dog, Sparky.

Kitty's son, Rob, has moved to the Ranch that his biological Father owned. He shared ownership with his father's best friend, Tex Duncan who was at the Rodeo when he died after being thrown from a bull. He and Tex have opened a Dude ranch operation and host people for a week or two week stay. It has proven o be a profitable idea.

One of the guests was Krissy Karr from Washington DC who came to the Ranch and she and Rob fell in love and got married on horseback. They now have two children. The oldest is called Skipper. His name is Robert Evan Harris. His little sister is called, Sunshine. Because she always seems to be smiling. Her given name is Roberta Kristine Harris.

Back in New Mexico at Trish and Kitty's little 30 acre Ranch, they call it. They still have two adopted children. They were nine and seven when they lost their parents to drugs. They have grown up to be talented in music and art.

Adam, the older has become a semi professional Musician. He has self-taught himself on the Guitar and gets some small jobs playing solo at parties.

His sister, Penny, has been able to produce works of art that the public likes and has been paying increasing prices for her work. She had an art teacher, Giorgio, for five years who was able to greatly increase her skill level.

They fell in love over time and when he asked for her hand in marriage Penny decided to end the relationship when she realized the age difference was too great to last. Giorgio died of a broken heart.

Trish thought about how her kids had grown up and left their home to start their lives. It was just her and Kitty at the ranch now.

Adam left for Nashville to pursue his music. He has a love interest now. She is from Viet Nam. Her name is Jenni. Her grandparents came to Texas following the fall of their homeland to the communist's.

They made their living working from a Shrimp boat. They were successful in spite of the harassment they took from the white shrimpers and fishermen.

After these people saw that her grandparents were good, friendly folks that would be willing to help them out in a pinch they relented and became friends with them.

Her father "Tommy", was a teenager when they arrived from Vietnam and growing up in south Texas he had to watch his eye for the local white girls that fascinated him.

He was an outsider and the white boys didn't like the idea of one of their girls being with a "Gook" as he was called. This to him was the same as a black man being called a "nigger". He hated it.

In spite of the racial differences he found a girl who fell in love with this young man. Her name was Darlene Minnich.

She was descended from immigrants from Germany who came here before the Second World War to escape the Nazi's. Her Great grand parents came into the States by way of New York City.

They soon left for the Midwest settling in Indiana for a few years before going south to Texarkana Texas. Their son, Franz, married a light skinned black girl from there named Patsy Mae Wilson. Her mother was white and her father was a black man named Jonny Odom.

Patsy took her mother's maiden name when her parents split up. Patsy married Frans Minnich and they had a daughter, Darlene.

She married Tommy and they have a daughter, Jenni.

Jenni and Adam met on the sidewalk in downtown Nashville one day and when she smiled at him with those brown eyes and long straightened brown hair that she wore down to her mid back he knew then and there that he had met his soulmate.

They went for coffee at a Starbucks. While sitting there he asked her,

"What's your name? Mine is Adam Flick and I am a musician. What brings you to Nashville?'"

Jenni replied,

"I came here from the Gulf coast of Texas to study at Vanderbilt. My name is Jenni."

Adam looked at her and said,

"You know what? You have the most beautiful eyes I have ever seen. Your lips just make me want to kiss them and your hair? I would love to run my fingers thru it."

Jenni laughed at that and said,

"You know what "Cowboy"? If you play your cards right you just might get a chance to do those things.'

They finished their drinks and left hand in hand. When they were outside, he asked,

"Where are you staying?"

She replied,

"I have an apartment off campus. Would you like to see it?"

Adam grinned and said,

"My, my, the lady asks, 'Would you like to see it?' He answered,

"In a New York minute."

They hailed a Cab and she directed the driver to her address. It was just short distance, maybe a mile. When they arrived she invited Adam to come in with her to see the apartment.

She went to the kitchen and got a pair of sodas from her refrigerator. They sat in the living room on her couch beside each other. They started with some small talk about where they came from and what they planned for their futures. Jenni told Adam,

"Like I said I grew up on the Coast. My parents are living there and he operates his Shrimping business that his father started when they came from Vietnam. My mother is a melato black with some German thrown in. So you see I am a mix of the whole world."

Adam replied,

"My parents both died when I was young from a bad batch of drugs. I and my sister were adopted by a Lesbian couple in New Mexico. They are both white and from the east coast. New York and Maine. They moved to New Mexico to start over as a couple. We lived way out in the mountains and had a pond in the back that we would swim, fish and go sail boating. We have several older step siblings that are half white and half Apache. The oldest died while in the CIA. His brother is a medical device designer in Kansas City. Their younger sister has a dog grooming place outside of Albuquerque. She has a wife too like our moms. They have been together for a long time. I don't know if they will adopt any kids like our mom's did. I think it would be a cool thing to do."

"WOW, you shared a lot more than me." Jenni said.

"Tell me about your sister. What's her name? And what's she do?"

Adam took a deep breath and let it out before he spoke,

"MY sister, Penny went thru a traumatic shock and she ended up in a facility to treat her depression. She has been there in treatment for the past two years. She will be getting out soon."

Jenni sat up and asked,

"What happened to her to cause this condition?"

He answered,

"She had a man who was older then her with whom she fell in love. He asked our Moms if they could get married. After they talked, Penny decided to call it off. He left that day and she never saw him again. He had gone home and died there. She felt that she caused his death somehow and she went into that deep depression that we were afraid she would be suicidal."

Jenni put her arms around Adam to comfort him because she could see a tear forming in his eyes. She responded,

"Oh, Adam that is so sad. I hope that she gets well and can restart her life. What did she do?"

Adam told Jenni,

"Penny is one of the most gifted Artist's that I have ever been around. The paintings she does look like they are alive. I hope she is able to continue to paint. The man who she loved was also her teacher for five years."

They sat for a while and then Jenni took Adams chin and tilted it toward her. She kissed him on the lips gently and then she leaned back on the couch so as to lay down. Adam followed her lead and laid down beside her. She was small next to him and they both fit on the couch. They continued to kiss and hold their body's close. Adam asked,

"Would you like to get more comfortable on your bed?"

Jenni got up and took him by the hand and led him back a hallway to her room. When they walked in they both started to remove their cloths.

Jenni could feel the heat on her face growing as she watched him finish the last of his cloths. They laid down on the bed and kissed again.

This time they both had their tongues exploring their warm mouths. She reached down and touched his growing manhood. She sighed an approval of what she felt. She gently squeezed it as it got harder.

Adam rolled her over on top of him and squeezed her small ass checks with both hands. She pulled herself up and with her hand she directed his into her warm wet pussy.

He let out a moan as he slid into her. She was tight even with as wet as she was. He laid and watched as she moved up and down slowly and rode back and forth. He hoped that he could last for a long time. He looked into her eyes as she rode him and saw her looking back at him. She picked up the pace and then when she was sure that he was about to cum too she had her release along with him.

They laid beside each other and cuddled. After a time she moved down Adams chest and sucked on his nipples. Biting them gently and licking them. She went down and licked his navel before getting closer to his now soft cock. She licked the end of it and put her hand on it to start stroking it back to a nice erection. She liked to lick the tip and gently suck it into her mouth. She could still taste a bit of his juice that had dried up after being wiped on the sheets. She didn't care about the sheets. He could leave "pecker tracks" anywhere at all. This beautiful hunk of man that she wanted so much to pleasure and make happy. She needed to be careful with what she was doing as she just wanted to get him hard again. Not to make him lose his load in her mouth. Not that she would mind. It was just that she still wanted and needed to get fucked again.

Adam got up and mounted her from behind, doggy style, his favorite and hers. They both liked to hear the slap of belly to ass cheek. It was like music to their ears.

Before he did he went down behind her and licked her pussy and ass to get her ready for when he pushed his now hard as a rock cock into her again and again and again untillll POP!

Jenni rolled over on her back, parted her legs and beckoned him to go down on her wet pussy and lick up all of their mixed juices. He gladly did. He licked the back of her smooth tan legs and worked his way up to her crotch. He moved his tongue along the legs until they became the edge of her pubes. He licked them on both sides and finally up to her clit. Adam sucked and licked her little pleasure spot and then thrust his tongue into her wet pussy. He rolled it around and around and Jenni enjoyed another orgasm while holding his head tight to her crotch.

Penny had just returned to her room from group sessions when she was called to the front desk. They told her that she had a visitor and she could meet them in the lounge area of the hospital. When she arrived there she saw Kitty had brought Ginger their Golden Retriever to visit today.

Penny was so happy to see the dog that she got down on the floor and hugged Ginger all the while the big dog's tail wagged up a storm.

She was so happy to see her again. And Penny to see Ginger. It had been a long recovery that Penny had gone thru.

The depression that she suffered after the death of Giorgio was so severe that she had even considered taking her life. The combination of the medicines and the counseling that she received had been an alleviating force and has helped to bring her back from a self-destructive path.

Trish and Kitty first noticed when she started cutting herself on her thighs and arms.

They were told by the councilors that she did this to punish herself for Giorgio's death. That she felt the need to cause herself pain for his pain.

The day was coming that she was being released from the Hospital and going home. She felt that she had been given the tools of recovery by the councilors to be able to get herself back to her life before depression. She would still need to take an anti-depressive but nothing so strong that would make her a Zombie.

On the way home she told Kitty,

"I want to get back to doing my art again. I do truly enjoy and need to get back. I know it will remind me of Giorgio, but I have learned how to control my anxieties and I am confident I can manage."

Kitty told her,

"We will take small steps at a time. There is no reason to jump Willy Nilly back into things. Just relax and get to know yourself again. The mountains and the trees are still waiting for you to get better. We know you can do it. Trish wants you to go visit Rob and Krissy at the Ranch for a little while before you come home. That alright with you. You can play with the little kids there. Skipper and Sun shine will warm your heart. They are both little sweeties."

Penny smiled and replied,

"I can't wait to see them again. It has been so long."

When they got back to the ranch, Penny and Kitty went in to the house and when Trish saw her she beamed and said,

"Welcome home baby. Did the trip go well coming back?"

Penny replied,

"Yes it was as long as usual, but I knew that when I got here I would feel safe with the two of you. Kitty said I can go visit Rob, Krissy and the kids. I would love to do that."

Trish smiled at Kitty and asked,

"When do you want to leave? Do I have time to pack a bag?"

They all laughed and the room sounded like it did in the past when everyone was happy.

Rob got the call from Trish that evening and was happy to hear that they were coming for a visit. He told Krissy, Tex and Ellen at supper that evening that they were getting guests.

Tex was happy to hear that Penny was released from the mental hospital. He said,

"That poor girl has been thru a lot and I hope she continues to get better. I was not all that happy when I heard about that man, Giorgio, getting involved with her. It really got me angered when he died and poor Penny thought it was her fault. I think she thought he committed suicide. The autopsy showed he died from a heart attack. Poor girl. Pass me the potatoes please."

Trish and family arrived on Friday afternoon and got settled into their rooms. After they all ate supper Rob suggested a short trail ride under the full moon. They all enjoyed the rides in the evening when the sky had just fallen from bright red sunset to the gray of twilight. To hear the lonesome call of the Coyotes as they called to each other let you know that you were in the West.

When they got back to the Ranch it was getting late so they all said their good nights and headed for bed.

Trish and Kitty laid awake for a while talking. Kitty said,

"Penny seems to be her old self again. Doesn't she?"

Trish replied,

"God I hope so. She really had me worried there before she went away. Giorgio was a mixed blessing in a way. He did make her a better Artist.

But then when they got involved romantically I cringed. I saw how much he meant to Penny. But I didn't want to see her get hurt. She was anyway."

Kitty replied,

"Yes, but we probably made a mistake of taking him into our beds too. You know?" Trish looked at her and then said,

"It was fun while it lasted. You have to admit you enjoyed it as much as I did. Even if we both knew it was wrong. He was an amazing lover. Wasn't he Kitten?" Kitty sighed and replied,

"You're right as usual. He did take the edge off of my sexual frustration. I'm not saying I am frustrated with our relationship. That is far from true. We have been in love ever since Maine all those years ago. We have stayed together and raised all our kids to be good people. And now the best is still out there. Kiss me my sweet."

Trish put her arms around Kitty and held her as she gave her a warm passionate kiss. They held their bodies close together and began to touch each other all over from shoulders to butts. Kitty could feel herself getting very wet and lovable as she sucked on Trish's warm tongue. Trish responded by reaching between Kitty's legs and giving her pussy a gentle squeeze. Kitty took a big breath and spread her legs as an invitation to Trish to give her some tongue pleasure. That was when Trish slid her hands down to Kitty's ass cheeks and while holding them she moved her face into Kitty's warm place between her legs. Trish put her tongue in Kitty's vagina and licked it fervently until she moved up to her clit. She licked and sucked on it all the while Kitty played with Trish's hair. She loved to feel Kitty's fingers going thru it while she was pleasuring her. Kitty experienced several orgasms before she let Trish go and moved over in the bed to let Trish lay down so she could be pleasured. After more than twenty years they both knew what they liked best. It was over an hour when they released their hold on each other during a sixty nine session that resulted in several more good orgasms for both. They kissed and went to sleep.

Tex and Ellen laid down in his bed and he stared at the ceiling for some time before she asked,

"What are you thinking about sweetie?" Tex put his arm around her and said,

"You know I think I am the most fortunate man in Texas right now. You want to know why?" She looked at Tex and asked,

"Why do you think that?" Tex replied,

"Because I am the only man in Texas that is going to make love to you tonight. Do you think that is why?"

Ellen parted her legs and let him place his big hands down on her pussy and run his fingers up and down her crack and in and out of her warm, wet hole. She gave him a kiss and then motioned him to lay on his back. Tex rolled over and Ellen moved over on top of him. She kissed him again and then moved down to take his cock in her mouth. She liked to suck Tex until he got really hard. She would then move up to ride cowgirl after lowering herself down on his cock so that it slid slowly inside her. He took a deep breath and let it out slowly as he glided inside her. She liked to rock back and forth and up and down while squeezing him with her vaginal mussels. They would do this position for a while and then she would lay on her side with him spooning her as he again slid it in. They could fuck like this for over an hour until they felt the urge to finish with an orgasm and ejaculation of his seed into her wetness.

When they were satisfied for the night they went to sleep with him still spooning her in his arms.

Rob and Krissy were up early with their kids. Skippy liked to run down to the horse barn and play with the pony that they still had from when their Aunt Katelyn came to visit. The Pony was her favorite until she out grew it. Then she liked to ride Rosie. She was Rob's favorite too. Sunshine was trailing after him as usual. He played nice with her, but was sometimes a little too fast for her to keep up.

Katelyn was soon to graduate from the University of New Mexico with her degree in Social Science. She wanted to become a Councilor so she could help kids like her sister, Penny. She saw how Giorgio's death had hurt her so much. She was sure there were other kids like Penny.

Her best friend Ashley Sweet had graduated the year before and Katelyn was asked to be her Maid of Honor when she and Freddy Odom got married. They all were close friends in college and she loved Freddy as much as she loved Ash.

They were getting married in Texarkana Texas so that Freddy's elderly Great Grandfather could attend. Jonny Odom lived nearby. His wife, Nancy passed away two years ago.

Freddy's Grandmother, Jonny's daughter Rita Moore lived near Biloxi Mississippi and she was coming to see her Grandson who was now a University Graduate with honors and he was getting married to this pretty white girl. She just knew they would make some pretty babies.

His mother Rose, lived near Clarksville Texas with a friend that Freddy never met but once who was a Preacher. She kept the Odom name as her mother had done when Rita's drunken husband ran off with her best friend.

Rose had Freddy out of wedlock and she too kept the Odom name for her son. She swore that he was going to be the best young man she could raise. She made damn sure he stayed away from the gang's that were around and kept him close so he studied hard and got straight "A's" all the way thru school.

He got an Academic scholarship to the University Of New Mexico. She was so proud of him she thought her chest was just goona "bust."

Rose asked Freddy,

"Would you like to have Preacher Dave to officiate at you all's wedding?" Freddy had only met her "Preacher Dave" one time. He seemed like a nice enough man so he told her,

"Sure Momma, if he would be able and you approve that will be O K. with me."

Rose was delighted.

Katelyn went to visit her brother Rob at the Dude Ranch. It had been a while since she had been there with school in Albuquerque. Now she had some time before she started grad school to get her masters as the next step towards her goal of being a Counselor. Having started college when she was only seventeen she was a bit younger than the others that were in her Masters Study group. Some were already working in the field.

When she arrived she saw Trish, Kitty and Penny were there too. She ran to Penny and put her arms around her and gave her a hug and a kiss on the cheek. Penny was excited to see her half-sister as well.

Katelyn had never met Tex's wife, Ellen and was happy to see that she was a good fit into their extended family. Katelyn had two weeks before her classes started so she just wanted to relax and have some fun on the Ranch. She went out horseback riding every day for several hours at a time. She really enjoyed her half-brothers property and could ride for hours and still be on his ranch. She got to know his kids too and was still new at being called "Aunt Kate".

Matt Frey was twenty seven and had graduated from UCLA. He was also in search of his Masters. He hailed from northern California near the Oregon border. He had gotten an athletic scholarship to UCLA for wrestling. Unfortunately during his first match he received a separated shoulder that shut him out from the wrestling program. The Coach told him that as a student athlete he would retain the scholarship grant.

"When we offered it to you we were after more than your muscles. We were after your brain as well. So just keep the grades up. You can come visit the wrestling room, but you will not be able to participate. Especially on the team. Good luck to you Matt."

At first he was disappointed, but he did as the coach told him. He buckled down and started to see his name on the Dean's list. His attitude brightened up a lot. He finished his senior year with a 4.0 GPA. The highest in the class.

He came from a Military family so he decide to enlist in the Marines for four years. They took him even though he had had surgery on his shoulder. He came thru the physical abuse of Boot Camp at Fort Pendleton in good shape.

He finished his enlistment and decided it was time to go back to school. He had a degree in Social Science and thought about getting a job working with troubled kids from the LA projects. He applied at University of New Mexico for his Masters. He arrived there on August first and the heat was worse than in California if that is even possible. He had an apartment just off campus and he could walk to class.

As he was walking in the class room he noticed a young girl who was in the same class as he. He looked her over and thought,

'How I wish I could just go over and touch her hand. It would be amazing.'

Katlyn picked out a seat in the room where she felt she could hear the Professor well enough and still be able to look out the window when it got too boring. She had just taken her seat when she looked across the room and saw this gorgeous hunk of muscle and good look's. It was Matt Frey.

He took a seat in the next row over from her so that he could see her whenever she turned his way. He already knew what infatuation felt like and he knew this was it. He just had to have her.

It was two weeks into the class that he finally got up the nerve to asking her out sometime. He was blown away. She said "yes" to a coffee break that afternoon.

Katelyn couldn't believe that an actual full grown man had asked her out. It was one of the greatest things that had ever happened to her.

They met at the local Starbucks for a Cappuccino and a Scone. She asked him,

"So, what is your goal from this class? I am looking at a career in School Counseling. I was home schooled up until college of course. One of my Mom's always had a shoulder for me to cry on if I needed it. I know there are a lot of kids who don't have a shoulder they can cry on. I want to be that shoulder. I have a sister that we were afraid was going to be suicidal before she got the care she needed.

He replied,

"WOW, there have been sometimes I wish I had a shoulder to cry on. As it is I have one good shoulder and one not so good. Wrestling injury in College. It didn't keep me out of the Marines for four year's though. There are no crying shoulders there I guarantee you. You mentioned, Moms, plural. How's that?"

Katelyn replied,

"Yes, I have two mothers. They have been together over twenty years and they are still in love. If you want to call them Lesbians, well that's what they are."

Matt replied,

"I see. I have no problem with that. How they want to live their lives is their business."

Katelyn told Matt,

"Well, all of us kids, and there are seven of us that grew up in that house and all went to college if we wanted to. We were home schooled and I started college when I was seventeen. My Brother, Rob inherited a five thousand acre Ranch in Texas from his Dad. One of my sisters started a Dog grooming salon with only a year of a business course. A brother was in the CIA and got killed overseas. His brother invented some kind of heart valve and lives in Kansas City. My youngest siblings are Adam, a musician in Nashville and his sister Penny is a very talented Artist."

Matt pondered what she said and then told Katelyn his story.

"My parents have a Vineyard in California and a winery too. My mother had inherited it from her father who had gotten it from his father. So the business has been in the family for three generations. I had to work hard all the time that I was growing up. There is always something that must be done on a vineyard. From pruning the vines to picking the grapes. We hired Mexicans to do most of the work, but I was out there toe to toe with them every day that I was not at school. I grew to hate the business even if it could make a lot of money. It was first and foremost a lot of work. Don't get me wrong, I am not afraid to work. I just decided to be my own man and not just inherit all the work that was there."

Katelyn said,

"I don't blame you Matt. That is a lot of work and I think you are right to leave it behind."

Matt replied,

"After seeing what I have seen in Las Angeles I know that I have a calling to go help those kids that are being forced into gangs and drugs and other bad stuff. If I can make a difference I want to do it."

When they left Starbucks Matt asked her,

"Where are you staying?"

She replied,

"My Mom, bought me a Town house here in town for while I am here and then I can sell it and use the money to do whatever I need to do. Or keep it for a Rental."

Matt thought about that for a moment and then asked,

"Where is your house?"

Katelyn replied,

"I am on my way there now. Would you like to ride along?" Matt said,

"Maybe next time. I have to get back to my apartment to feed my dog."

Katlyn asked,

"What kind of dog do you have?"

He answered,

"It's just a mutt that I picked up along the street. It had no collar and it looked hungry. So what was I to do? Just walk away? Not my style. So now Sly is my constant companion when I am not at classes. Or soaking up coffee at Starbucks. See you tomorrow."

Katelyn's heart was racing when she got to Patty's Grooming salon. She pushed the door open and announced,

"I'M IN LOVE!!"

Patty and Tina looked up at her and asked at the same time,

"WHO's the lucky girl? Or is it a real guy this time?"

Katelyn told them about Matt and how they had coffee together. Patty pushed the Cavalier St Charles that she was working on away and got up to hug Katelyn. Tina kept working on the Afghan hound that she was occupied with. He was a show dog like their Sparky. Patty took Katelyn by the hand and led her into the office. When they got there she told Katelyn,

"Take a seat sweetie and tell me all about him."

Katelyn started be saying,

"His name is Matt Frey from California and he was in the Marines for four years. He lived on a vineyard up north. Hated it and decided to go to college to get into the same line of work that I want to do. He is in my class at the University. We went out for coffee at Starbucks and spilled our guts about family.

I offered to take him over to my house but he had to go feed his dog. Isn't that sweet?"

Patty nodded and said,

"He does sound like a keeper. Couldn't be seduced, A? Well that's nice. Says something about him. Maybe he's gay. Hate to see you take his pants off on the first date."

Katelyn laughed at her and replied,

"Now that's something you might do. Especially if Tina could hold his arms to keep him from fighting you two off. Don't tell me you wouldn't bring some poor soul in off the street and have your way with him. I'm not even going to bring him over here to be introduced. HE'S MINE!"

Donnie Brill had just gotten off the Bus that brought him back to Albuquerque from the State prison where he has been housed for the past five years for just messing up some lesbian's Dog grooming place. He mused to himself.

'They want to see a hate crime. I'll show them what a real hate crime looks like next time. While I was in there I got raped or beat up by Niggers or Spicks every other day. I'm gonna get me some of them too. I hate them Spooks and Spicks. They will pay for my pain. I will pay a visit to my favorite Gay church again. This time it won't be rocks. I know about Molotov Cocktails now.'

Ellen told Kitty,

"I'm not going to be as cute like Krissy was with her pregnancy announcement. You remember, The March Hare from Alice with the pocket watch and saying, "IM LATE IM LATE". Instead I am going to just say, 'Everyone put your arms up. Now anyone who is not pregnant put your hands down.' Then I will be the only one with my hands up. Won't that be fun?"

Kitty laughed and said,

"MAYBE, you will be the only one with your hands up. Who else do you think it might be if there if another pair of hands stays up?"

Ellen replied,

"It's not you is it? I know that Trish was hoping that she could have a baby. But I don't think it is her."

Then Ellen said,

"I guess we will see when we all get together. Are all your girls from Albuquerque coming here for the Fourth of July party? I'll bet it's one of them."

Donny Brill watched as the Bus dropped off some more people in front of the African American cultural center where there was going to be a celebration of the signing of the Civil Rights Bill in 1964. There were a good number of White and Black and Hispanic families who had already entered the building. He watched as the last ones entered. He waited for about a half hour before he carried out his attack.

He walked up to the front door and lit the rag that was stuffed into the neck of the wine bottle that he had filed with gasoline. He watched as people milled around tables of food and listened to a local band playing.

Then he tossed the bottle into the air and watched as it came down and broke open spuing flaming gasoline on the floor and on several people who were standing near where it broke.

Pandemonium broke out and people started screaming and running for the doors.

Donny ran across the street and watched as the fire spread to anything in the way. There were several fire extinguishers in the building and some of those inside managed to get them and proceeded to fight the flames. In a few minutes they had the fire out.

Someone had called 911 and both Fire and Police arrived at the same time. They questioned the people to see if anyone saw who tossed the fire bomb. A little eight year old boy who was standing at the front of the room saw Donny come in and toss the Molotov cocktail. He was able to give the Police a pretty good description. He noted that it was strange that someone was wearing a hoody that time of year. He also had a mask on so that he could only see enough of the man's face to tell he was white.

Katelyn went to class that day and was happy to see Matt standing by the door to the class room. He smiled at her and said,

"Hi Katelyn. Are you ready for the big test today? I studied all weekend and my brain is fried. I didn't think this was going to be this difficult." Katelyn replied,

"I studied for it too and it all just seemed to come fairly easy. Maybe we should study together next time."

Matt thought about it for a second and replied,

"That sounds like a plan. Want to hit the Starbucks after class? We can talk about getting together for a study date."

Katelyn almost turned inside out with glee at hearing Matt suggest a DATE. Even if it was just to study,

"We can go to my place. I have a lot of room to spread out papers and books. It has a nice kitchen to make something to eat. I had two great cooks to learn from growing up. So I can make us a meal when we get there and we can study in the evening."

Matt said,

"I am looking forward to it. For now let's just get past this test today."

Katelyn smiled at him and they walked in the room together.

Patty and Tina had just finished up the last of the dogs they had scheduled for the day and the last owner had arrived to pick up their pet.

They closed the shop and headed for home. They were tired and in need of a shower.

Sparky enjoyed going to the shop every day with them. He liked meeting the dogs that came in for grooming service.

When they arrived home they took him out in their enclosed yard to do his business before going in the house. He ran around the yard a few times to stretch his legs and then he pooped and peed. Now for his supper.

Tina was the first to hit the shower and Patty was not far behind. With the water running as hot as they could stand it they proceeded to lather each other up as they always did.

Patty liked the feel of Tina's hands working all over her body. When she reached between her legs Patty parted them so that she could get all her girl parts as clean as a girl can be. She did the same for Tina.

Patty asked Tina,

"Shall we go to bed and play for a while or should we eat first?" Tina replied,

"If we eat now we will have all evening to play. I would like that if you agree to it."

Patty said,

"How about we play now and have supper and play again?"

Tina agreed. She took Patty's hand when they got out of the shower and toweled her off and powdered her dry skin with baby powder so she smelled good. Patty did the same for Tina. They headed for the bed adjacent to the bathroom.

When they laid down Tina had her head on a pillow and Patty put her hand on Tina's leg and ran her fingers up and down it until Tina put her hand on Patty's and guided it toward her center. With her hand embracing Tina's pubic mound they kissed and Tina pulled Patty over on top of her. She said,

"Let's do what Lois showed me that time. Remember? We cross our legs so that our pussies are touching and then rub them together and push in and out."

Patty replied with a smile,

"O K, I like that. Then we can do what we like the best. You can be on top to start and then the next time I will take top."

They got in position with Tina's left leg over Patty's right leg. Patty had her left leg over Tina's right so that they were in a scissors position. They could see their clits and vaginal openings matched up and ready to move. They did some bumping and then they rubbed their pussies across each other. I t felt good and they knew from experience they could both attain an orgasm from rubbing their wet parts together.

They played like this for fifteen minutes or so and then switched to sixty nine with Tina on top and Patty on the bottom. Patty liked to be able to hold Tina's ass while she licked her pussy. She could use her hand to run it across Tina's opening and make her squirt sometimes. Patty liked it when she did, even if it made a little mess in the bed. It was worth it.

Donny watched for a while and then walked a block over and got in his car and went home. He was disappointed that no one was killed and only a few suffered burns. He thought,

'Next time I will have to plan ahead and make sure there are no fire extinguishers for them to use. When I do the Lesbians this time I will just fire bomb them like the Niggers. Only I won't fail like I did with them.'

Katelyn and Matt left the campus and headed toward her house that was only a mile or so up the road. When they arrived she parked in the driveway and they walked around back and entered the back door. She liked to go in this way better then thru the formal Livingroom. It just seemed cozier to her. It went right into the kitchen. Alongside the kitchen was a dining room that went to a staircase that went to the second floor where the bed rooms were located. They stopped along the way and picked up a Pizza to have for supper.

After supper they worked on some of the things they had been assigned by their professor. They were told that there were some things in that material that would be helpful for when they had to put together their Thesis.

Katelyn said,

"I don't think I will have much of a problem putting mine together. I am just going to use my own experiences growing up in a blended family of Natural, Foster and Adopted kids. How that dynamic shaped who I am and how it will help me in my career in social work."

Matt replied,

"You do have a lot to draw on. I have a dysfunctional family in some ways. In other ways it all seemed normal. I guess that it was my fault that it seemed dysfunctional. I rebelled at working on the vineyard when I was fourteen and didn't like the way my father and mother treated me afterwards. That was why when I left College I joined the Marines. I have a couple Uncles who were Marines. Anything to keep from going home."

They ate the Pizza and talked for a while when out of the blue Matt asked,

"Katelyn, would you mind if I gave you a kiss? I know I am being a bit forward but I can't stand seeing you and not showing my affection for you." She replied by moving over to him and putting her arms around him. He kissed her on the lips and she was receptive to his warm tongue in her mouth.

They kissed like that for a short time when he reached around her back and under her sweater and unhooked her bra. She raised her arms so he could remove the sweater. Then she took off his sweatshirt and then they kissed as they found a way to remove their pants.

They were down to their under pants and panties. She took his hand and led him to her bed. He laid her down gently on her back and pulled her panties down her legs. He dropped his to the floor. He got down on his knees at the side of the bed and pushed her legs up so he could kiss and lick the back of her legs. He did this to both legs and licked his way up to her crotch.

She remembered the first time Freddy Odom did that. It felt good then and it did now. She liked it when Ashley did it too. Right now she was just going to focus on how Matt was doing it. He was so slow and deliberate when he licked her clit and went down slowly until the tip of his tongue was just at her opening.

He slowly pushed his tongue in her and put one of his fingers inside her vagina. He pushed it in and rubbed her "G" spot while he was sucking on her clit. The more he rubbed it and sucked it the stronger she felt her orgasm happening.

When the first one past she pulled Matt up so that she could have him enter her with his stiff cock. He obliged and when the tip had entered he stopped and pulled out and then pushed back in. Little by little he went deeper until he had pushed all the way in.

Katelyn squeezed her vaginal muscles tight around him and then relaxed. She liked to do this as she knew it would give him a good feeling. When they had done it missionary for a time she pushed him off and said,

"My turn on top, O K?"

Matt rolled onto his back and she mounted him cowgirl style and held his cock so that she could guide it directly into her wet pussy again.

This time she rode him slowly pulling up so the tip was just inside and then slowly lowering herself back down. She kept this up until she could see in his face that the end was coming soon.

She picked up her speed and it was not long before she felt the warmth of his release inside her. She laid down on top of him and he held her in his arms. They fell asleep.

Freddy Odom was so excited to be getting married to Ashley that he was beside himself. He had invited all his Frat House Brothers to the wedding. Only a few could accept as they lived too far away to attend.

His Mother, Rose Odom was excited too. Her son had not only graduated from the University, but had a job offer in Dallas. Only a few hours away from her.

Her Mother, his Grandmother was excited also but for another reason. She wanted a Great grandchild and she just knew that it wouldn't be long before she could be holding him or her in her arms. She was not the least bit concerned that the baby's mother was white.

She had seen the result of inter-racial mating's before and she thought they were the prettiest children around. Her own Grand Daddy, Jonny Odom had a girl child with his white wife Barbara Wilson. Her Mother Rita was from his black wife, Nancy.

Rita always wanted to have a white mother. But she was just black on black and that was who she was. She was just as happy as could be when Freddy announced that he was marrying a white girl from college.

Donny waited for the women to leave the grooming salon that evening and he followed them to where they lived. He watched as they got out and went in the house. He waited around until it got dark.

He watched as the upstairs lights went on and then a half hour later they went out. The only light then was from a TV in the bedroom. After the eleven o'clock news was over that went out. He waited until midnight so that he was sure they were asleep.

He got out the Molotov cocktail he had made and walked up to the front door. He peered in and with a flashlight he searched for the stairway to the second floor. His idea was to set the fire in the living room where the stairs were so that they couldn't get out that way and would be forced to jump from the upstairs if they even woke up before the flames reached them.

He turned the bottle upside down to allow the gas to run down into the rag that was the wick.

When he did some of the gas spilled on the sleeve of his hoody. Some splashed on his pant leg as well. He stood at the front door and as he lit the rag the vapors from his pant leg and sleeve reached the flame at the same time.

He dropped the bottle and it broke on the porch and engulfed him.

His screams woke the girls and they smelled the gasoline and saw the flames on the porch.

Patty called 911 to report the fire. Then they ran down and went out the back door with Sparky.

The Fire Department got there in fifteen minutes and were able to extinguish the fire on the porch and found a scorched body there with a broken wine bottle nearby.

There was still some fingers left on its left hand that allowed identification of Donny Brill. They linked him to the other fire-bombing the week before.

Patty was relieved when she found that it was him that had vandalized her shop before. She thought that it was sad that he had to lose his life because he was so hateful of some other groups.

She and Tina went to Church that Sunday and prayed for his poor soul.

Kitty took her new Grandchildren back up to the Ranch in New Mexico for a couple weeks so that she could have them close to her and Trish while they were still very young. It seems that kids are born and the next thing they are off to College.

While there they took them out on the sail boat every day and Skipper liked to catch fish. Sunshine liked to play with the old Golden Retriever, Ginger. The dog liked the attention and enjoyed chasing the ball when it was thrown.

While they were there Kitty got a call from her brother Jack. He told her that Evelyn and he were lucky to have survived a boating accident on the high seas. They decide to take the Insurance money for the lost Lobster boat and start over in something that had a solid footing instead of a rocking deck.

The cold snowy winters in Maine were catching up with them and they decide to move south and open a Bait and Fishing Tackle shop along the Gulf coast and wondered what Kitty thought about the idea. She said,

"You ever hear about something called a Hurricane? They happen pretty frequently along that coast. You know Texas has a lot of inland lakes that are not totally immune to storms but they are usually a lot less damaging. And I'm sure there are places for a Bait shop." Jack thought about what she said and then replied,

"You know what little sister? You are still pretty smart about some things. This is one of them. I am going to look at Texas and find a place to call home. It will be hard leaving Maine with some family still there but Evelyn and I have had enough."

Kitty replied,

"Why don't you two come on down and stay here for a while until you find a spot. My son Rob and his Partner know a lot of people over that way and can probably hook you up with a good deal. There are a lot of large lakes out west of Austin. Like Lake Buchannan and Lake Travis."

Jack said,

"We'll think about your offer to stay with you guys until we can get settled somewhere. Talk to you later, love you sister, Bye now.

Kitty replied, "Love you to. Talk again later."

When she hung up the phone she turned to Trish and said,

"That was Brother Jack. He and Evey are abandoning Maine for a warmer place. They lost their boat in a storm and with the insurance money they are looking to open a bait shop somewhere warm. I told him there are a lot of lakes in Texas that would probably have room for another bait shop. I told him they should come here to stay until they find a place to settle."

Trish replied,

"That sounds fantastic. I have never met your Brother but I know he cares a lot for you and you for him. Of course they can stay here. Love to have them."

Penny loved to watch the sunset up on the mountain as the colors changed from blue to red to a golden orange mixed with yellows. She liked to try to match those colors in her work. She had done a series of paintings where she would do one and then turn her vision so that the next one was at the edge of the first. Making a panoramic series from the one place where she set up. She did this at different times of the year to pick up on the different colors that prevailed.

In late winter when there was still snow on the high places and the Aspin were still bare skeletons of themselves. The rocks and fallen logs were able to be seen on the ground.

One day as she was working on a painting a young woman walked up the mountain with her little dog. She stopped to watch and chat with Penny. She was an attractive Apache about thirty years old. As they chatted she told Penny,

"My Sister is an Artist too. She likes to do portraits of our old people on the Mescalero Reservation. She has sold a number of them down in Santa Fe." Penny replied,

"Oh really? My adoptive Brother married a girl from that reservation. They live up in Kansas now. I don't get to see them very often. They come down maybe once a month for a weekend. That's about it. Her name is Brenda. She lived with her Grandmother on the reservation after her mom died. What's your name?"

The woman replied,

"My name is Ronnie Davis. I moved from the reservation when I went to College in Santa Fe. I went to Saint John's College for my bachelors, a liberal Arts degree. I applied and was accepted to Southwestern College for my Masters. It was in Counseling and Art Therapy. I heard about you in my travels and wanted to meet you. I understand you suffered a loss in your life and it left you in a world of hurt. I understand it took a while for you to recover from it. Can I ask you about your recovery? I know we have just met, but your Mom's said I could talk with you if you are willing."

Penny looked at Ronnie and after a bit she asked,

"What would you like to know?"

Ronnie replied,

"Has your Art helped you to stay focused away from the pain you experienced?" Penny responded,

"I have been home now for some time and I feel that it does help me. The man who helped me to fully develop my talent was the cause of my problem. We fell in love and when the romance dissolved and he left I was heartbroken. He died shortly after that and I felt responsible for his death. Which was ridiculous. He just had a heart attack, not my fault. Let's move on, please." Ronnie looked at Penny and then asked,

"Do you still have feelings for him?" Penny replied,

"NO, I have recovered from the hurt and I have moved on. I do not have an active love life at this time and I am alright with that. I live here with my mom's and I enjoy painting and then taking my work to town to display it for sale."

Ronnie asked,

"Would you go with me to Santa Fe to meet my Professor and tell her how your recovery and life are doing with your Art as a means of copping with your grief?"

Penny looked at her and without hesitation said,

"When would you like to go? I can pack up a few things and we can be on our way today if you like."

Ronnie smiled at Penny and told her,

"You sure are an enthusiastic girl if I do say so. Let's go talk to your Moms and let them know what we are doing. O K?"

Penny packed up her supplies and easel and headed down to the house. When they arrived she told Trish and Kitty that Ronnie wanted her to go with her to Santa Fe to visit her professor so that she could ask her about how her Art has helped her to return from the dark place she was in following Giorgio's death. The women thought about it for a moment and then Trish asked Ronnie,

"This isn't something that is going to possibly set her back is it?"

Ronnie told her,

"No, I think she has enough recovery time to be past any loss of progress. I wouldn't ask her to do this if I thought it would."

Kitty asked,

"How long will she be there?"

Ronnie said,

"Only a day or two. I want to have her visit the Campus in case she ever wants to pursue a career in counseling herself."

Trish told Ronnie,

"She doesn't even have a bachelor's degree to be able to attend a Masters course. I don't know if she wants to do that. She got a lot of help from the professionals at the Hospital she was at and has a deep respect for them."

Penny said that she did indeed respect them, but really did not want to pursue that as a career. With that she looked at her moms and said,

"So can I go with Ronnie?"

They agreed that it would be alright for her to visit Southwestern College for a few days.

She packed up a few changes of clothes and they were on their way by noon after a light lunch with Trish and Kitty. Ronnie was very interested in how Penny came about being raised by two women.

On the way she asked her and Penny replied,

"When my Brother and I were young our parents both died from a drug overdose. We became wards of the state as we had no other relatives to go to. Kitty and Trish were contacted by Children's Services and we were placed in their care as Foster kids. They later adopted Adam, my Brother and I. We have been here ever since. We couldn't have found a better home to live in."

"Has the fact that they are Lesbians had any effect on you or your brother?"

Penny said,

"We get that a lot. No, we have had a very happy home to live in and they have been the most loving parents that we could ever ask for. I do have an older sister who is married to another woman. They are happy together and have a dog grooming shop near Albuquerque. So I guess that a girl can fall in love with whoever they want. Whether it's a man or another woman."

She asked Ronnie,

"Do you have a boyfriend or do you have a girlfriend. I am going to guess the latter. Am I right?"

Ronnie replied,

"Guilty as guessed. Your "gaydar" is pretty well tuned. We have been together for over a year now. She was from Dallas and came to the College for her Masters too. Her name is Jamey and she is twenty six. She is a mixed race girl whose father was Black and her mother was Asian. They met in College too. Jamie is a very sweet girl who is 5'-6" tall and has a lighter shade of skin, kind of like bronze. I guess. You will meet her at our house."

The rest of the trip was made up of small talk. When they got to Santa Fe they stopped for supper at a Red lobster. Penny enjoyed the trip and the meal. They headed over to the house that Ronnie and Jamie shared. It was about two miles from the Campus.

Jamie met Ronnie at the door with a kiss. Penny followed her in and smiled at Jamie. She looked Penny up and down and then told Ronnie,

"This is the prettiest girl that you have brought home in a long while. That last one was the super model from San Angelo Texas. She was a doll, but this gal is no slouch. Hi my name to Jamie. Pardon me if I gush. That's just my personality. Ronnie probably already warned you about me."

Penny laughed and said,

"That's alright. I am usually on the quiet side until I get to know someone. She failed to tell me that you are so pretty. I love the color of your skin. I am an Artist and I take notice of skin colors of people. She told me you are mixed race. I have three siblings who are half Apache and white. They tend to be a shade lighter than bronze. So when their parents were killed in a car wreck they were shunned on the reservation for having a white mother. That's how they got to be in my family. My Mom's adopted five of us. There are two more who just happened to get born into the family."

Jamie and Ronnie took all this in and then Jamie remarked,'

"She has an interesting past. Makes you wonder where she may go."

Ronnie asked,

"Do you mean career wise or orientation wise?"

Jamie looked at Penny and then just asked her,

"You are a big girl. Which way do you think you will want to swing?"

Penny looked up at the ceiling before she answered.

"Is this what this is about? To see if I am interested in your lifestyle choice? Perhaps I am. I have never been kissed or done anything else with a girl." Jamie asked,

"Would you like to try it?"

Penny looked at her and without any warning she grabbed Jamie and kissed her on the lips. Jamie pushed her away and said,

"Ronnie and I are a couple and although I would like to bed you sometime I don't think it is appropriate to just up and kiss me like that."

Penny was embarrassed and replied,

"I'm sorry I just had to do that. I wanted to feel what it was like to kiss a girl. I am sorry if I offended you or acted out of place."

Ronnie told Penny,

"That's O K. I like to watch when Jamie is making love with another woman. She likes to watch me too. So don't be embarrassed for what you did. It happens all the time. When you meet my Professor you will be amazed at how beautiful she is for a Tran's woman."

Penny's eyes went wide and her mouth dropped open.

"Are you serious? I have never met a Tran's person before."

Ronnie told her,

"You are in the big city now country mouse. You may see and hear things you have never encountered before. Let's sit down and talk for a while about things."

Penny nodded and took a seat at their dining room table. Jamie sat across from her and Ronnie sat at the end. Ronnie started the conversation by asking Jamie,

"Tell us how you lost your virginity. I know the story but I think Penny will like to hear it.

Jamie looked at the other two and then she said,

pushing his cock inside me. It went in slowly and when he had the whole thing in I felt him let go with his load. He didn't know then how to control his ejaculation back then. Believe me he knows now. He told me that he just thinks about something else. Sometimes he can just think about mowing the yard and trimming the edges. Doing this he said he can last for a half hour or more. Depending on who he is fucking. She looked at Penny and said,

"Your turn Country Mouse. Tell us how it happened."

Penny sat there with her hands in her lap thinking about when Giorgio had first taken her virginity up on the mountain side in the daytime on top of the table. As she thought about it the feelings came flooding back. The sensation of his hands on her naked skin. The feeling of his tongue on her girl parts. How wonderful it felt when he did it. Then the feeling of his cock sliding inside her. Finally she spoke,

"It was the most amazing thing that ever happened to me and I do truly miss him. "

Ronnie and Jamie sat and looked at Penny and then Ronnie said,

"That is precious Country Mouse. Tell me about you're feeling about girls. Have you ever had any thought about how it would feel to be in the arms of another female?"

Before Penny could reply Jamie asked,

"Do you ever taste your own juices down there? You know when you masturbate."

Now Penny said,

"Yes I do fanaticize how it would feel to be with another girl. They are so much softer than boys and men. Yes, Jamie I do masturbate like all girls do and boys to. I have seen my Brothers bed sheets. The answer is yes I have tasted my juices and I like them. I suppose that most all girls taste alike."

Jamie asked

"Would you like to find out? There are two of us that you can do a taste test on if you want to find out." Penny looked at Jamie and said,

"I have never done this before so you will have to guide me so I do it right, OK?"

With that all three got up from the table and Jamie led the way to their bed room.

When they got there Ronnie was the first one naked. Jamie was not far behind.

Penny started to remove her cloths. She looked at the two naked women laying on the bed in front of her and she could feel herself getting very turned on.

They started kissing and fondling each other's breasts. Penny watched with interest while she removed the last of her cloths. She got up on the end of the bed and watched as the other two laid on their backs and parted their legs.

Penny could see both of their open and wet pussies. She moved up closer and put her finger on Ronnie's clit and watched her face as she gently rubbed it. She put a finger on Jamie's clit and worked both of them at the same time it brought a smile to all three of them.

Penny moved closer to Jamie and touched her tongue to Jamie's leg where it touches her pubes. She licked there for a minute before moving into her vagina.

She licked it and pushed her tongue in as far as it would reach. She went back up to her clit and sucked and licked it until she felt Jamie having an orgasm. She decided it was time to service Ronnie. She did the same treatment that she gave Jamie. Then Ronnie told her,

"O K you did good. Now it's our turn to pleasure you Country Mouse."

Penny moved over to let the others get up off the bed. She moved over front and center.

Ronnie went first and pushed Penny's legs up to her chest. She went down on her pussy and followed on down to lick her anus. She spent a lot of time there as she knew how good it felt.

She let Penny's legs go back down as Jamie climbed on to get a face job. Penny was amazed at how these woman could give her some of the most amazing orgasms of her life.

The other two let her sit on their faces as well so that she could get as much experience as they could deliver.

Before the night was over they introduced her to scissoring or 'tribbing' as it is also called.

It is where the two women cross their legs so that they can rub their wet pussies together. Rubbing their clits and feeling their wetness can bring them to an orgasm sometimes if not every time. This comes from reliable sources.

The next day Ronnie took Penny over to the College to meet her Professor. When they entered her office Penny was amazed at how everything looked. The Professor walked in a minute later and shook Penny's hand.

It took a minute for it to register what Ronnie had told her yesterday that this is a Tran's woman. Penny looked her over and noticed her breasts. They were a nice size and shape. Her hair was brown and hung down below her shoulders.

She had a nice figure thanks to the hormones that she had been taking for several years. She was in her forties, but could pass for thirty. Penny wondered if she had the final surgery.

Ronnie introduced her to Penny,

"Penny, this is Ms. Donna Dixson, she is the Department Head. She has been here for the past fifteen years and knows more about Art Therapy then anyone on the planet. She has several PHD's in phycology and Social Science. Ms. Dixson I want you to meet Penny Flick from up north around Magdalena in the mountains. She had been in treatment for deep depression with suicidal tendencies for nearly two years. She has been discharged for some time and she is an excellent Artist who has sold many of her paintings in Magdalena as well as up in Taos. After watching Ms. Frick for the past several days at her home and then in my home. I truly feel that her Art work is helping with her depression. My Partner and I have seen that she can be made happy and contented by Lesbian activity, which she says is a new thing in her life. Whether she ops for the lifestyle or not is up to her. We have shown her that she can be happy on that side of the street, meaning being a Lesbian. She has two Lesbians as her parents since she was seven years old. It is not a life style that is foreign to her.

The Professor looked at Penny and then asked,

"Are you happy with your life right now or is there something that you would like to do that would make you happier or more contented?" Penny looked from Ronnie to the Professor. Then she replied.

"Yes there is something that I would like to do that will make me more contented and happy. That thing is to have my own Art Studio and teach the techniques that Giorgio taught me to younger student so they can have similar success like me."

Brother Adam in Nashville has met a girl who he has fallen for. Her name is Jenni. She comes from the Gulf Coast and is the daughter of a Vietnamese immigrant and a mixed race woman. She is drop dead beautiful and it is not wasted on Adam.

He has invited her to come and hear him play at a Club in Nashville. A local band picked him up to replace their Guitar player who left town suddenly and left the band short a key player.

Adam auditioned for the spot and got it. The pay was not too bad either. The Head of the band told Adam that he had bookings in town for the next five weeks and then he was heading to Dollywood for a week. He was able to give Adam work for six weeks. He hoped that there would be more gigs coming. Adam liked the guy and enjoyed playing with a band. He mostly played on the street or for parties as back ground noise.

Jenni showed up at the Club with a couple of friends from College that liked Country music. After all this is Nashville. They arrived shortly before the band was to start playing and Adam saw them in the audience. He smiled and waved to Jenni and her friends.

They started playing and the band was known to do a lot of Garth Brooks songs.

Everyone enjoyed them and when they played "I've got friends in low Places" the whole room went wild. The girls had a lot of fun and decide to become "Groupies" and follow the band around town while they were playing here.

Maybe even get lucky some night when the band was Horney.

Jenni was waiting when the evening came to an end at two a.m. Adam packed up his Guitar and they walked out to her car. They loaded it up and headed for her place.

They got there and went inside. Jenni poured them each a cold Ice Tea. Adam liked that better than sodas. Sodas made him burp.

Jenni had some news to tell Adam. Her parents were coming up from Corpus Christi to visit for a couple days. She wanted him to meet them.

Her Mom and Dad liked country music and was sure that they would like to hear Adam play. She was right.

They arrived at her Place on Friday afternoon and Adam had a gig that evening.

She took them out for supper and then to the Club to hear him play in the band.

They enjoyed the evening and then they headed back to her apartment after the club closed. They were impressed with Adam and thought that Jenni had found a nice young man.

He came over to meet them the next day when they could spend more time in a quieter environment than the Club. He told them his family history and how he and Penny were adopted and grew up in New Mexico.

Jenni's mother asked him,

"Did you have any harassment growing up with having Lesbian mothers? It was probably good that you were away from the town or cities at that time."

Adam replied,

"No, it was never a problem. They are very independent women who took no disrespect from anyone. They have been the most loving and supportive parents any child could want. There were seven of us kids in the family and we all got along together. Most have gone on to College and have been successful in life. My brother Rob has a big Ranch west of Huston."

Jenni's Dad asked,

"What happened to your parents?"

Adam told him,

"They both died from a drug overdose we were told. We went to Trish and Kitty at first as foster care and then they adopted us. Best thing that could ever happen."

Her dad said,

"It sounds like you are right. Jenni should bring you down to our home some time. I will take you out on one of our shrimp boats. You like shrimp?"

Adam smiled and replied,

"I sure do Sir. Right up there with Barbequed Pork ribs."

Her Dad laughed and said,

"A man after my own heart. My wife here can do up some of the finest ribs you will ever eat. She grew up in a mixed up family like ours, except her mom was a half black and her dad was from German emigrants and was as white as could be. I am from Vietnam so Jenni has a varied racial background. But ribs are a favorite at our house.

Adam replied,

"Yeah, my Moms were raised in the Northeast and they learned how to cook Pot roasts at a young age. My mom, Trish lived in New York and had a Nanny that taught her how to cook. Mom Kitty, was from Maine and knew how to do sea food."

They continued to chat into the evening and about ten o'clock Jenni's mom and dad said that it was their bed time.

Her dad said,

"We'll see you two in the morning. Our long trip and the time at the club is catching up with us."

Jenni and Adam said good night to her parents and they all went to bed.

After she and Adam were in her bed they talked for a while about how her parents seemed to like Adam. He said,

"They are really nice people. You picked a good pair to be your parents."

She laughed at that and said,

"Luck of the sperm I guess. I could have been a boy and ended up on the shrimp boat from the time I was six years old like my Dad. Instead I didn't go on the boat until I was twelve. That was when I decided to go to College instead so that I didn't have to work on the deck of a boat."

Adam asked her,

"You never have told me what your major is at Vanderbilt."

Jenni told Adam,

"I am in my senior year of an Accounting program using computer science to generate profit and loss generations that can predict the future of a business and how that business can get to that level. It bases that projection on past performance and the local market."

Adam said,

"That sounds complicated. Why not just go into brain surgery or something simple like that?"

Jenni looked at him and smiled,

"Let's just forget about it and just make love."

With that she kissed Adam and put her arms around him. Adam responded by putting his hand on her pussy and giving it a gentle squeeze. Jenni gave a little moan as she continued to give him her tongue. He could feel his cock getting harder. She reached down and held it in her hand. Stroking it gently she asked,

"Would you like me to suck you off a little bit before you get inside me?"

Adam grinned and said,

"Only if you let me lick your pussy for a bit more than a bit. Like until you cum. Will that be alright with you?"

She replied,

"How about if you let me suck you all the way until you come too. Would you like to cum in my mouth or between my tits?

Adam was really getting Horney with her talking dirty to him.

He suggested,

"Why don't we just do it sixty nine? I'll let you be the top that way when I cum you can decide what to do. Spit or swallow."

She replied,

"You know I always swallow unless you want me to share it with you in a kiss."

Adam let her turn around and put her crotch over his face with her legs parted so he could get right where he needed to be. He put his hands on her small ass checks and massaged them while he licked her small girl parts. She shaved her pubic hair so the she really did look like a twelve year old girl except for her tits. She must have gotten that gene from her mother's black background. Surely not from her father's Vietnamese genetic factor.

Adam enjoyed having sex with Jenni and thought that he just might be falling in love. He had not ever felt what he was feeling now. He was also feeling that he was about to squirt his load. She had the gentlest way of using her tongue on him and it was working. He felt like his ass was turning to stone as it got nearer and nearer to the finish line. He grabbed her pussy in his mouth and shook it back and forth and he muttered,

"I love you Jenni."

As he felt his ejaculation happen. She moved up and down on him as she sucked every last drop of essence from him.

They both laid there as their passion waned and they decide to go to sleep and finish what they have started in the morning.

In their minds they both knew that this was a special time and it was going to be a life changing moment.

In the morning Adam had her mount him cowgirl way and she rode him to another warm planting of his seed. He watched her eyes as he flowed into her. They both knew that they had just started a family of their own.

Her parents left for home that afternoon and promised Adam that they would love to have him and their Daughter come to visit them in Corpus Christi.

The day of Freddy and Ashley's wedding was getting near. She invited Katelyn to come down to stay with her at Freddy's Mom's house to get ready for the big day. Ash was going to be wearing a beautiful off white dress that had a train that was ten feet long. It had poufy shoulders and a conservative neckline. Katelyn's dress was a pastel green and was floor length.

Rob and Krissy and the kids were coming for the wedding and staying at a local motel. Tex and Ellen came along with them. Trish and Kitty came with Patty and Tina.

Katelyn thought,

'Wow, that's most of my extended family. I wonder who all will come to my wedding. Probably have to have a partner first. Which way should I swing? I really like a man, but I kind of like girls too. OH, Ash, you have confused my mind.'

It was the night before the wedding and she, Krissy, Ellen, Trish and Kitty had a bachelorette party for Ash.

Kitty and Ellen went to a Liquor store and got several bottles of Yellow Tail Wine. They had a local Caterer come with a mix of snacks and sweet treats. Fancy cheese and crackers.

They had a good time and made fun of Ashley. Fitting condoms on a bratwurst and laying it between a pair of wrinkled up prunes. They put a hole in a large peach and stuck the Brat in it. The women drank all the wine and it was after midnight when they called it a night.

Ash and Katelyn went to bed. They had shared a bed on many occasions in College. They thought that after tonight they would not be sleeping together again.

They would go their separate ways in life and possibly not see one another again. Oh no, they would still be able to visit some times.

Katelyn did have deep feeling for Ashley. She had feelings for Freddy too. He had been their first time and he had made a bond with both of them. Perhaps they should explore Polyamory. She turned over in the bed and asked Ashley,

"I am thinking about something that I don't know how you will take it."

Ash asked,

"What's on your mind?"

Katlyn replied,

"I am thinking about having a Polyamorous relationship with you and Freddy. Do you think he would be up for it?"

Ashly's eyes went wide and she replied,

"We can ask him and I'm sure he would love to have you as his side girl. You can be my side girl too. Wouldn't that be great?"

Katelyn kissed Ash and said,

"We would be a "Throuple". Even if we live apart we can get together when we can and share our love for each other. I like the idea. Let's propose it to Freddy tomorrow after the wedding. Or, do you think we should break it to him now?"

Ash looked at her and asked,

"What's his number? I'll call him now."

Katlyn said,

"It's only two thirty. You think he is still awake?"

Ash said,

"I don't know if he had as much to drink as we have but if he did he is probably asleep like we should be. Now give me a good kiss this time."

She did and with their mouths open they had their tongues exploring each other. Ashley put her hands on Katelyn's ass and squeezed it. Katlyn responded by putting her hand down on Ash's pussy. She wiggled her middle finger in her hole and bent her finger to rub her "G" spot. Ash said,

"Let's move over so we can sixty-nine."

Katelyn smiled and said,

"I was just going to suggest that myself. You want top or bottom?"

Ash told her,

"You can take top this time. I'll do it next time."

The next day the wedding went off with no problem. The bride and the groom both had a slight hangover from the Bachler parties the night before.

Rob had a couple beers but Tex had a diet coke. He has been sober for over thirty years and attends AA meetings on a monthly basis. It has helped him to stay sober.

He fell off the wagon a time or two right after his best friend, Rob Harris, Rob's Father was killed at the rodeo when thrown from a bull.

He had told Rob that he needed to watch his drinking. He even told him that if he wanted to he would take him to a meeting.

Rob said that he only drank beer and he didn't drink to get drunk. He could also leave it alone if he wanted to.

Tex never pressed the issue with him. He had told him a long time ago about losing a close friend to whiskey. His friend was driving drunk when he had a car wreck that killed his girlfriend. He committed suicide shortly after. Tex was crushed.

Freddy and Ashley headed for New Orleans for their Honeymoon. They stayed at a bed and breakfast in the French quarter and fucked their asses off. She asked him about including Katelyn in their relationship. They both love her.

Freddy thought about it for a while and then told Ash,

"You know what? That's a good idea. And you are right, I do love her as much as I do you and if she was here right now I would let you watch as I fucked her right here in this bed."

They both laughed and Ash got back on top to ride him like a horse.

Freddy said,

"Then I can watch you two go at it with that kissin' and pussy licken'. It would make my old cock stand up and want to join in."

Ashley laughed and told him,

"Yeah, you would like to watch wouldn't you? If we saw that you were hard again we would both jump your bones. You got the sweetest cock around. I would sit on your face awhile she would suck your sweet cock until you pop your load."

Freddy grinned and asked,

"Do you want to sit on my face right now?" Ash moved up in the bed and straddled his face while she placed her hands on the head board to hold on. Freddy did a good job on her and he had her getting one orgasm after another for a half hour. He reached back and jerked off while she kept him busy with his tongue. They were both ready to go back to the real world after a week in the City. The food is great and the sex was magnificent.

Patty and Tina asked Trish and Kitty about how they went about adopting a child. They felt they were ready to be parents.

They were told to see the children's service office in Albuquerque. They were sure they could help.

They would do an investigation of them first before they would recommend an adoption. Their best way would be to get a child thru Foster parenting. That was the way they got Adam and Penny.

Tina told them,

"I have not told you my back story. I have not even told Patty. I was in the "system", foster care that is, for most of my life. My mother was a meth head and she gave me up when I was three. I was starting to be a problem when she brought the Johns home. She didn't want me to see what she did to support her drug habit. My dad was a drunk and left her right after I was born. He went back to the Reservation and he was never seen again. I was in one home after another. I didn't get along with some of the other kids there so they just kept pushing me along to another town and another house. Finally when I aged out of the system at eighteen I hit the streets. It was not long after that when Patty found me. She gave me a job that I love and now we have a beautiful house that we can raise a child in."

Kitty looked at Tina and said,

"I am sorry to hear that you had a bad experience with the system. It is broken in some places but the people there do try to do their best for the kids. Sometimes I guess that some just fall thru the cracks. We adopted Patty and her brothers when they were orphaned. We will do everything we can to help you get a child."

Trish looked at Patty and told her,

"You have really made me a happy mom. Being able to start your business and expand it like you have. Your unexpected good fortune to have met Lois Lawrence when you did. And her kindness to bequeath to you all her stuff. House, cars and her sweet dog Sparky. I just know he would like to have a playmate in the house."

Ellen told Tex that she was ready to go to the hospital. If they didn't get there soon she was going to have this little girl there in the ranch house.

He told her that would not be a problem. He and Harold and the other cowboys had helped birth calves and foals so they could probably handle some little girl child.

Ellen said,

"That's O K, I still want to be somewhere that I know that they know what they are doing."

Tex smiled at her and said,

“Get in the car and we will be there in fifteen minutes or so, it’s only thirty some miles to North Cypress Hospital.’

“You think I want to go a hundred twenty miles an hour your wrong. I can hold her in a little bit longer if you just drive sensibly.”

Tex was O K with that. She was in a hurry to get there. He was just trying to help. It took about forty minutes to get there to Ellen’s satisfaction. They went in and it was only fifteen minutes until Tex was Daddy to a six pound four ounce daughter. He didn’t smoke, but he handed out cigars to everyone he met.

To be a father when other men his age were sending their kids to College was O K with him and Ellen. She was a lot younger then Tex.

While Trish and Kitty were up to visit Patty they decided it was time to go to the Hospital and get their annual mammograms. They have been consciences about getting them as Trish’s mother died young from breast cancer. They had made appointments earlier that week so they could just walk in at the appointed time. Kitty went first and with the three dimensional X-Ray machine it could find the very earliest signs of a tumor.

Then Trish got her’s done. They waited for the results of the X-rays. The Dr. came out to the waiting room and called Trish to follow him in to see the pictures that were taken of her right breast. It showed a spot about the size of a pea. He explained that at that size they would do a biopsy to determine if it was malignant. She asked him if it could be done that day as they had traveled a long distance to get there. He said the best he could do was that afternoon about four o'clock. Trish told him that was fine. They waited at Patty's shop until it was time to return to the Hospital for the biopsy.

After the biopsy was done the Dr. reported to Trish that it was indeed malignant.

He said that they would do a "lumpectomy" to determine how far it had spread. They did that the next day and they found that it was a type of cancer that was confined to the one breast and it was not likely to be in both.

They discussed the next option. The cancer cells were found on the edges of the sample that they removed. They would have to do another lumpectomy.

That also showed more cancer cells. They conferred with Trish and Kitty and together they decided to have a bilateral mastectomy in case the cancer would eventually spread.

They scheduled the surgery to be done in two days so they made arrangement to stay at Patty's house.

Trish would be in the Hospital for about five days until the healing was starting and the stitches could come out. She had to admit they had done a magnificent job of making them almost invisible. Now she wanted to schedule a restoration surgery. To do this they told her that they take fat from the belly and move it up to where the breasts were. It is a major surgery and has its risks.

Tex and Ellen came home with the new baby. Robs kids were excited to see their new 'cousin'. She was named Rachel Gloria Duncan. They gave her their grandmothers' names from both sides of the family. She is being breast fed and Ellen is a good source of milk.

Dear reader,

There has been so much that has happened in Trish and Kitty's lives and their family that I may have to write yet another chapter. I hate to do it because someone may pass away and it would make me cry, again.

Sincerely,

R. L. Atkins

CPSIA information can be obtained
at www.ICGtesting.com
Printed in the USA
LVHW111946180123
737433LV00003B/29

9 781685 471545